CAN PUP FIND THE PUPS?

Vincent X. Kirsch

I Like to Read®

HOLIDAY HOUSE • NEW YORK

Tate likes to draw.

He likes to draw Pup.

Can you see five drawings of Pup?

Tate looks for new things to draw.
Pup looks too.

Tate sees new things to draw.
Pup sees five pups.

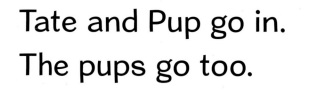

Tate and Pup go in.
The pups go too.

Tate sees dinosaurs.
Pup can't see the pups.
Can you?

Can you see six dinosaurs?

Can you see the five pups?

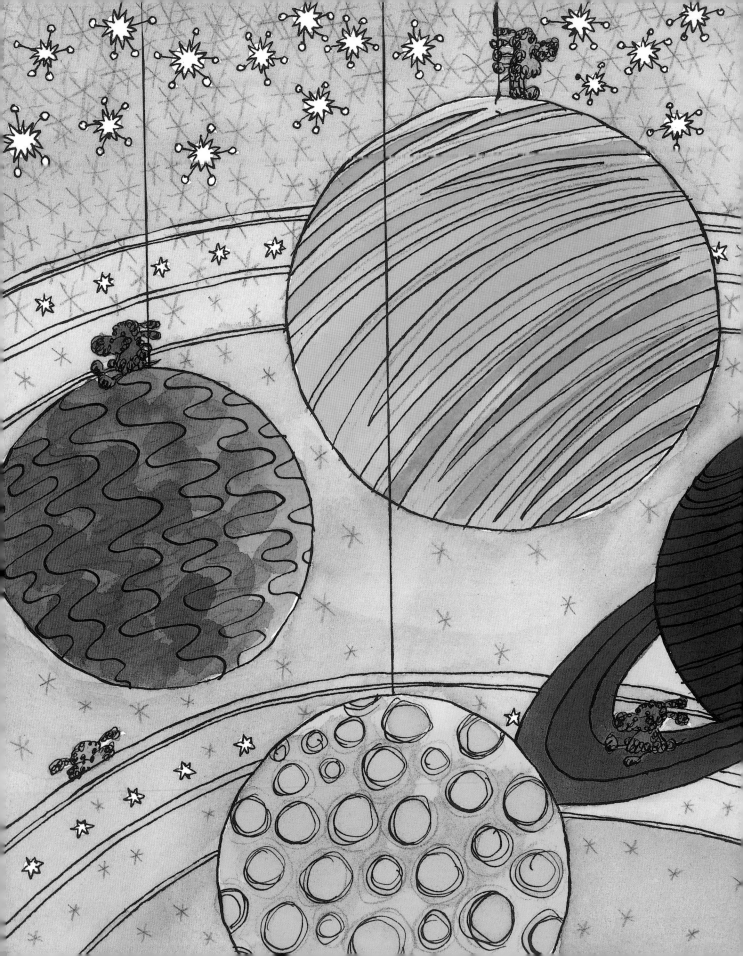

Tate sees planets.
Pup can't see the pups.
Can you?

Can you see eight planets?

Can you see the five pups?

Tate sees butterflies.
Pup can't see the pups.
Can you?

Can you see ten butterflies?

Can you see the five pups?

It is time to go home.
Pup can't see the pups.
Can you?

Tate is thinking.

Pup is thinking.

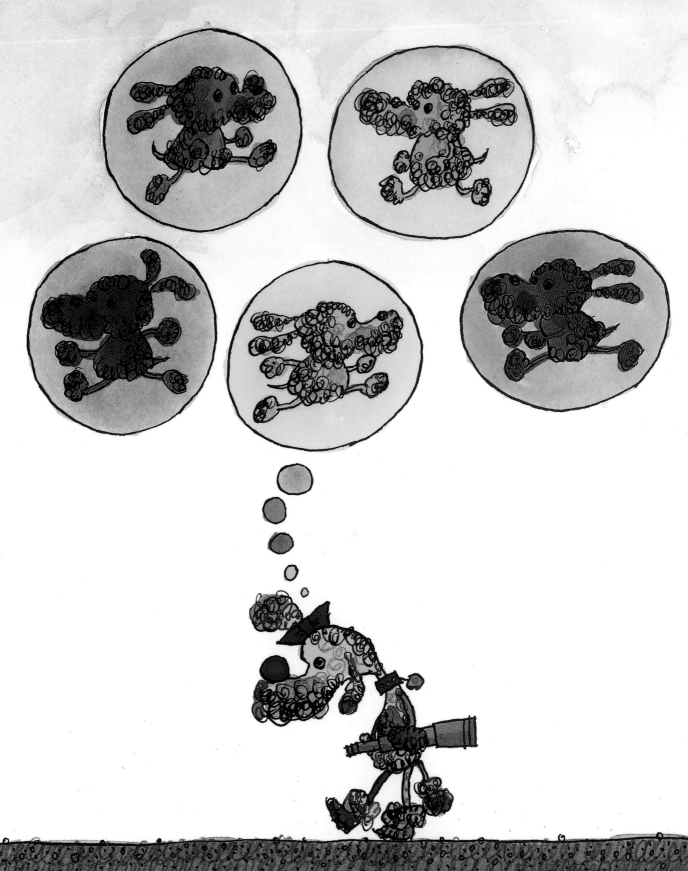

Tate sees five pups.
Pup sees them too.

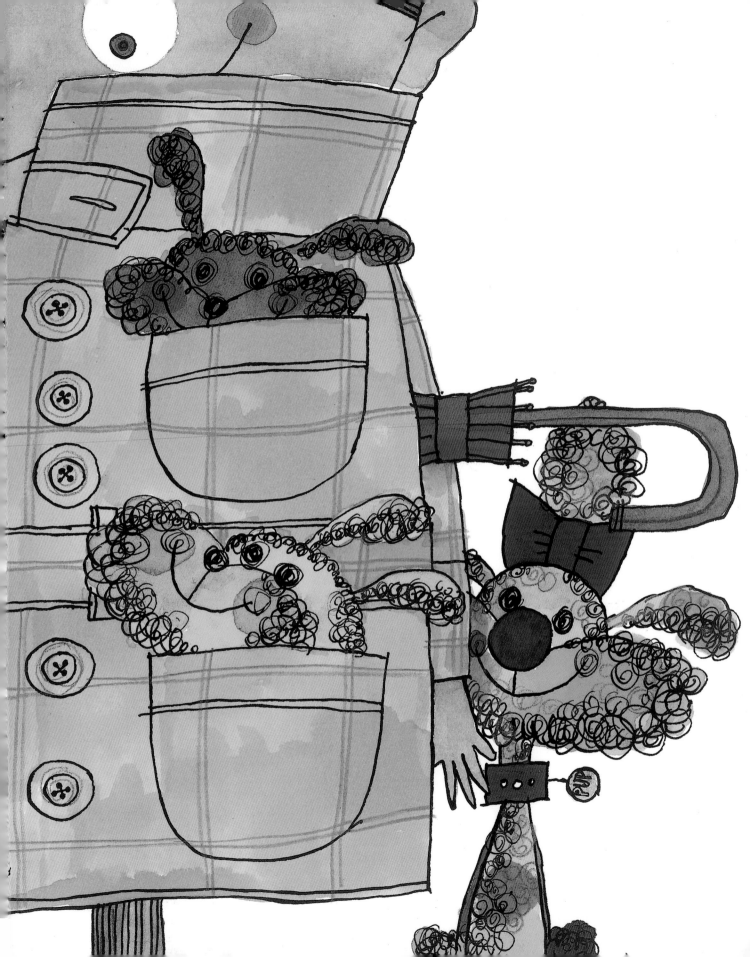

The five pups have a new home.